LITTLE CRITTER®'S
THE PiCNIC

BY MERCER MAYER

A MERCER MAYER LTD. / J.R. SANSEVERE BOOK

PUBLISHING

1997 edition published in the United States by GT Publishing Corporation,
16 East 40th Street, New York, New York 10016.

What a nice day
for a picnic.

Dad says this
spot is good.

Yikes! Too many bees.

Dad says we will find
a better spot.

This is not a good spot.
This spot is too wet.

Dad says he knows
another spot.

He says this looks
like a good spot.

Oh, no! Too many cows.

Dad says we can have
a picnic over there.

"Hello!
Is anyone home?"
asks Dad.

Uh-oh!
Too many bats.

Dad says he knows
an even better spot.

He says it is
the best spot of all.

Dad is right.
This is the best spot.

What a nice day
for a picnic,
after all.